WHISPERS
TO MY SOUL

WHISPERS
TO MY SOUL
AWAKENING THE INNER VOICE

The Sacred Space Press

The Sacred Space Press

WHISPERS TO MY SOUL

Awakening the Inner Voice

Copyright © 2025 Abigail Henry

ISBN 978-1-7640433-1-1

First Edition

Printed Worldwide

For more information, visit: thesacredspacepress.com

Cover and interior design by Abigail Henry

With deepest gratitude, I dedicate this book to those who have walked beside me with love, truth and unwavering support.

To my children, your love is the compass of my heart. Your light has awakened me in ways I never knew possible. Thank you for inspiring me to grow, to heal and to stand fully in who I am. You are my greatest joy and my most precious gift.

To my husband, your open heart has supported me with strength and love through every chapter of our journey. Thank you for walking beside me - with courage, tenderness and compassion. Our journey is my home.

To my sister, my lifelong cheerleader, thank you for knowing me from the very beginning, for standing beside me with unwavering love and for believing in me. Your support has meant more than words can express.

My sacred circle, thank you for your open hearts and for receiving what I have shared - through words, energy or teaching. In holding space to express and explore, you helped me grow. You have been both students and mirrors, a gift I deeply treasure.

Each of you has shaped this journey in your own sacred way - and for that, my heart is full.

About Me

My journey with divine energy has carried me across continents, but one truth has always remained clear: to hold space for others in remembering who they truly are - through sacred healing, inner reflection, self-discovery and soulful awakening.

For decades, I have worked with Reiki, intuitive energy healing and spiritual mentoring to help others release emotional blocks, realign with their soul's wisdom and reconnect with their inner light. As a Reiki Master, Practitioner and Teacher, I have had the honour of mentoring others on their unique spiritual paths, holding space for balance, clarity and peace to emerge.

My spiritual path is both intuitive and ancestral - rooted in a lifelong relationship with energy and emotion, shaped by my maternal grandmother who read tea leaves and my paternal grandfather who practiced ancient folklore healing. Their gifts and traditions continue to guide my work and deepen my connection to the unseen.

Tarot has long been a trusted companion in my spiritual practice - a mirror to the soul that brings clarity, guidance and gentle affirmation. It continues to inform the way I connect with energy, intuition and the subtle whispers of inner truth.

After publishing *The Tarot Journey: Affirmations, Mindfulness Colouring and Soul Journaling with the Major Arcana*, I felt called to offer a new kind of experience - one that goes beyond the cards and directly into the heart space. *Whispers to My Soul: Awakening the Inner Voice* was born from this calling. It is a sacred invitation to pause, listen and honour the quiet wisdom that lives within you.

Wherever you are on your path, know this: you are not walking it alone. I am honoured to walk beside you. May these pages be a sanctuary for your healing, your remembering and your radiant becoming.

With Love, Light & Laughter

Abigail

Soul Whispers Pathway

Welcome
◇ Navigating Your Soul Journey
◇ Creating Your Sacred Space
◇ Whispering Your Intentions to the Universe

The Soul Journey
Each Soul Whisper invites you into deeper connection with yourself. Through sacred affirmations, creative expression, rituals and reflections, you will awaken your inner voice, stir the wisdom within and gently unfold into the truth of who you are.

◇ "I Am" Affirmations
◇ Mindful Mandala Colouring
◇ Signature Mini Ritual
◇ Soul Reflection
◇ Soul Whisper Section Overview

The Soul Whispers:

➡ #1. Affirmations 01-07: **I Am Grounded** - Stability, Presence, Trust
➡ #2. Affirmations 08-14: **I Am Open** - Creativity, Flow, Emotional Ease
➡ #3. Affirmations 15-21: **I Am Empowered** - Confidence, Courage, Boundaries
➡ #4. Affirmations 22-28: **I Am Love** - Compassion, Connection, Self-Worth
➡ #5. Affirmations 29-35: **I Am Expressive** - Truth, Voice, Self-Expression
➡ #6. Affirmations 36-42: **I Am Aligned** - Clarity, Discernment, Insight
➡ #7. Affirmations 43-49: **I Am Connected** - Trust, Peace, Sacred Awareness
➡ #8. Affirmations 50-52: **I Am Whole** - Integration, Expansion, Soul Completion

The closing Soul Whisper 8 (Affirmations 50-52) brings together the energy of all that came before - inviting you to embody your growth, honour your voice and step fully into your wholeness.

Additions
- Journaling Space for Further Reflections
- Bonus - Extra Mindful Mandala Colouring Pages

Navigating Your Soul Journey

This book is a companion for your soul - a space to return to yourself, soften into your truth and realign with what matters most.

Whether you choose to move through it in a steady rhythm or follow your inner guidance moment by moment, *Whispers to my Soul* is here to meet you exactly where you are.

The book is divided into eight Soul Whisper sections, each one holding a collection of "I Am" affirmations centred around a deeper energetic theme. Across these eight sections, you will find fifty-two affirmations - one for each week of the year or to explore in your own sacred timing.

Each affirmation is paired with a mindful colouring mandala, a mini ritual and a soul reflection prompt, creating a multi-sensory space for connection, healing and insight.

You are invited to move through the journey in the way that feels most true for you:

◇   **The Weekly Rhythm**
You may wish to journey through the book one page at a time, allowing each affirmation to hold space for your week. Let it be your anchor. Begin each week with the featured affirmation and mini ritual. Reflect on the soul prompt, explore the mandala with mindful colouring and revisit the words as needed throughout the days.

This path creates a sacred rhythm - one of integration, softness and slow unfolding.

◇   **The Intuitive Flow**
Alternatively, allow your soul to lead. Open the book at random, trust the message you land on and receive it as a whisper from within. The perfect affirmation will find you when you need it most. This approach honours your inner wisdom and offers guidance in divine timing.

There is no right or wrong way to journey here. You may even blend both - setting a rhythm while remaining open to spontaneous insights. Trust your own sacred unfolding.

Come as you are. Breathe. Colour. Reflect.
Let the pages be both a sanctuary and a mirror, returning you to the still voice of your inner mandala.

Creating Your Sacred Space

Before you journey inward, it helps to tend to the outer. Your sacred space is a physical reflection of the inner sanctuary you are cultivating - it is where intention meets presence and where the outer world softens enough for your soul to be heard.

Your sacred space does not need to be elaborate. It might be a quiet corner, a cozy chair, a windowsill bathed in morning light or simply a place where you can pause, breathe and be. What matters most is how it feels: nurturing, safe and aligned with you.

Here are a few ways to create your sacred space:

◇ **Clear the Energy**
Begin by gently cleansing the space. You might use sound (a bell or soft music), smoke (sage, palo santo, incense), or breath and intention to clear old energy and invite in the new.

◇ **Set the Mood**
Bring in soft elements that speak to your senses - cushions, blankets, candles, crystals, essential oils, plants or natural objects that ground and soothe you.

◇ **Choose Anchors**
You may wish to include symbolic items like herbal tea or objects that carry spiritual or personal meaning. Let your space reflect your spirit.

◇ **Keep it Simple**
Your sacred space can be temporary, changing or mobile. It is less about aesthetics and more about creating a space where you feel safe to exhale and reconnect.

◇ **Make it Yours**
Let your sacred space be an invitation - to slow down, to soften, to listen. You are not just decorating a corner of your room. You are preparing a sanctuary for your soul.

Return here often. Breathe here. Reflect here.
Let this be the place where your inner mandala begins to unfold.

Whispering Your Intentions to the Universe

Every journey begins with a whisper - a calling from within to realign, reconnect and remember. Setting an intention is like lighting a candle in the heart of your experience. It does not need to be loud or elaborate. It just needs to be true.

Your intention is not a goal to strive for, but a gentle compass. It anchors your energy and opens the space for meaningful transformation. As you move through these pages, let your intention be a sacred thread that weaves clarity, presence and purpose into your unfolding path.

Take a moment to pause and breathe deeply. Let the noise of the world soften. Bring your awareness to the quiet truth within you.

Ask yourself:
◇   What am I calling in right now?
◇   What does my soul need most at this moment?
◇   How do I want to feel as I journey through these pages?

Let whatever arises be enough. Trust the words, images or sensations that come. You may choose to write your intention below or simply hold it in your heart.

My intention for this journey:

Keep this intention close. You may return to it or revise it as you grow.

You are exactly where you need to be.
Let it be your guide. Your anchor. Your light.
Let the journey begin.

"I Am" Affirmations

At the heart of this book are fifty-two "I Am" affirmations - gentle Soul Whispers designed to help you reconnect with your inner voice, the part of you that knows, feels and remembers. These affirmations are the threads that weave through each page, offering both structure and spaciousness for your inner journey.

Each whisper is simple, yet powerful. The words "I Am" carry an energetic weight that grounds you in the here and now. They act as an anchor, drawing you out of the noise of the world and back into your centre. These statements are not about striving or self-improvement. They are about softening into your truth, returning to the wholeness that has always lived within you.

These affirmations do not ask you to become someone new. They invite you to remember who you are. With each breath, each colouring stroke, each reflection, you gently peel back the layers of distraction and reconnect with your soul's quiet knowing.

Spoken regularly or explored intuitively, these soul whispers become guideposts. They help quiet the mental clutter and emotional noise so your inner voice can rise - clear, calm and heard. This is the voice of your intuition, your wisdom, your essence.

Throughout this book, you will journey through each affirmation, thoughtfully paired with a mindful colouring mandala, a gentle ritual to embody the energy of the phrase and a soul reflection prompt to support deeper connection and insight. Together, these practices create space for healing, integration and transformation.

You can choose to move through these pages weekly, creating a sacred rhythm and gentle routine. Or you can use them intuitively, opening to the page that calls to you in the moment. There is no right or wrong way - only the way that feels true for you.

Speak them aloud. Whisper them into your breath. Let them move through your body and settle into your energy field. Allow them to ripple into your day and root into your being.

These are not just words. They are invitations. They are echoes of your soul.
They are the awakening of your inner voice. our voice is ready to be heard.

Mindful Mandala Colouring

Each Soul Whisper in this book is paired with a Mindful Mandala Colouring, carefully chosen to reflect the energy of the affirmation it accompanies.

These mandalas are not simply beautiful patterns; they are sacred mirrors. Each one carries the frequency, flow and feeling of the affirmation - helping you to anchor the energy not just in your mind, but in your body, your heart and your spirit.

As you colour, you move beyond thinking into being. You create space for stillness, reflection and subtle healing. The very act of slowing down, choosing colours intuitively and moving your hand with intention allows the soul whisper to root more deeply within you.

The Mindful Mandalas Colouring are here to:
✧   Ground and embody the energy of each "I Am" affirmation
✧   Activate creative flow and soften the busy mind
✧   Support emotional release, calm and clarity
✧   Anchor your inner work into a tangible, sacred practice

You do not need to be "good" at colouring. You do not need to plan, perfect or overthink. Simply choose colours that you feel drawn to - trusting that your intuition knows exactly what is needed.

Some days you may colour a little, others you may lose yourself in it. Both are perfect.

This is a sacred act of presence. A quiet meditation. A creative offering to your soul. Let the shapes, lines and spirals become a container for your energy. Let the colours you choose be a reflection of your inner landscape. Let the mandala anchor your affirmation into the beautiful energy of your being.

Your "inner mandala" is a symbolic and spiritual concept that refers to the sacred, centred space within you - the calm, wise and intuitive part of your being that holds your deepest truth and inner peace.

Signature Mini Ritual

As you journey through *Whispers to My Soul*, you will notice that each soul whisper - each "I Am" affirmation - is paired with its own Signature Mini Ritual.

These mini rituals are simple, nurturing practices designed to help you embody the energy of each affirmation. They create a sacred moment of pause, intention and connection - helping you move the words beyond the mind and into your breath, your body and your soul.

Each ritual is unique to the affirmation it supports. Some will invite you to use breathwork. Others will guide you to place your hands on your heart, light a candle, move your body or simply sit in stillness. All are gentle. All are optional. All are there to deepen your experience if and when you feel called.

The Signature Mini Rituals are here to:
◇   Anchor you into the present moment
◇   Awaken the inner voice connected to that affirmation
◇   Support the energy shift each whisper invites
◇   Create a bridge between reflection, embodiment and everyday life

You are welcome to spend as little or as much time with the rituals as you wish. Some days you may feel called to sit with them fully; other days, a single deep breath with intention may be enough.

This is your journey. Trust your rhythm.

When you pause to engage with each ritual, you allow the affirmation to settle more deeply within you - awakening not only the mind, but also the heart, the body and the soul.

Each whisper. Each breath. Each ritual.
A gentle awakening of the voice within you.

Soul Reflection

Alongside each affirmation, mindful colouring and mini ritual in this book, you will find Soul Reflection's.

These prompts are invitations - small sparks of insight designed to help you gently explore your inner landscape. They are not tasks to complete or questions to get "right." Instead, they are open doorways, encouraging you to listen more deeply to your own truth.

Each Soul Reflection is carefully chosen to align with the energy of the corresponding affirmation.

The Soul Reflections are here to:
- ◇ Deepen your connection to the whisper's meaning
- ◇ Awaken your intuition and inner wisdom
- ◇ Encourage self-inquiry in a nurturing and empowering way
- ◇ Offer space for emotional release, clarity and soul discovery

You may choose to journal your reflections, speak them aloud, meditate upon them or simply sit quietly and feel into the answers that arise. There is no right or wrong way to engage - only what feels authentic for you in the moment.

Sometimes a prompt will ignite an immediate insight. Other times it may plant a seed that blooms days or weeks later. Trust the timing of your own unfolding.

These Soul Reflection prompts are not about seeking perfection. They are about honouring your process. They are about allowing your inner voice to whisper, stir and rise.

At the close of each Soul Whisper section, you will find dedicated journaling space, accompanied by a Soul Whisper Reflection Overview - three thoughtfully crafted prompts inviting you to pause, integrate and witness how the chapter's themes have stirred within you. These overviews gently support your path of embodiment, offering a sacred space to honour your growth and deepen self-awareness.

Pause. Breathe. Reflect.
Let the spark within you guide the way.

I AM GROUNDED

SOUL WHISPER 1
STABILITY, PRESENCE, TRUST

I Find Safety Within

This affirmation is a sacred reminder that your deepest safety begins within. No matter what chaos surrounds you, you can return to your body, your breath, your centre. Safety is not something we must seek from others – it is a state we cultivate through self-trust and presence.

This whisper invites you to soften, to create an inner sanctuary and to rest in your own care. When you know how to hold yourself gently, life begins to feel less threatening. You are your own anchor. You are your own safe space. Let this knowing rise and steady you.

I AM
Safe In My Breath, My Body And My Becoming

Signature Mini Ritual

Make yourself comfortable and wrap yourself in a soft blanket or shawl. Breathe deeply and place your hands over your heart and belly. Whisper the affirmation three times with the exhale.

Soul Reflection

1. Where in my body do I naturally feel a sense of safety or calm? How can I anchor into that feeling more often?

2. What daily practices help me reconnect with my breath and remind me that I am safe just as I am?

3. When challenges arise, how can I honour my journey of becoming, without abandoning my inner sense of safety?

ALLOW YOUR SOUL TO SPEAK WITHOUT OVER THINKING

I Trust The Ground Beneath Me

This affirmation invites you to lean into now - the only place where life truly happens. So often, the mind races ahead or loops back, but this moment holds more than enough. It offers breath, stillness and subtle support. Even when things feel uncertain, you can find a thread of calm by returning to what is.

The present moment doesn't demand that you fix or understand everything - it simply asks you to be. This whisper reminds you: you are not alone in this moment. Life is here. You are held. You are supported.

I AM
Supported By The Present Moment

Signature Mini Ritual

Sit or stand barefoot on the floor. Visualise roots growing from your feet into the earth. Say the affirmation as you inhale and exhale.

Soul Reflection

1. In what ways does the present moment offer me support, even when life feels uncertain?

2. What helps me trust the unseen foundations - the "ground beneath me" - during times of change or fear?

3. How can I deepen my connection to the present moment as a source of strength, rather than something to rush through?

ALLOW YOUR SOUL TO SPEAK WITHOUT OVER THINKING

Stillness Is My Sanctuary – I Return To It With Ease

This affirmation brings you into the quiet spaces within - the ones that remain unmoved no matter what storms arise. Stillness is not the absence of motion, but the presence of peace beneath the motion. When you allow yourself to slow down and listen, you touch something eternal.

This whisper encourages you to anchor in this inner calm, where clarity lives and your nervous system can exhale. In the stillness, your spirit speaks, your body softens and your truth becomes audible. You don't need to chase anything. Be here. Be still. Feel yourself gently held.

I AM
Anchored In Stillness

Signature Mini Ritual

Light a candle. Sit for three minutes in silence, following your breath. Repeat the affirmation silently each time you exhale.

Soul Reflection

1. What does stillness feel like in my body, mind and spirit - and how can I welcome more of it into my daily life?

2. When life feels overwhelming, what gentle rituals or reminders help me return to my inner sanctuary of stillness?

3. How has embracing stillness helped me hear the quieter truths within me that busy moments might drown out?

ALLOW YOUR SOUL TO SPEAK WITHOUT OVER THINKING

My Body Is My Home – I Treat It With Kindness

This affirmation is an invitation to return to your body as a sacred dwelling - not just a vessel but a wise, living temple. In a world that often pulls us outward, this affirmation gently calls you inward, grounding you in presence and self-compassion. To be at home in your body is to listen to its signals, honour its rhythms and embrace it with tenderness, just as it is, in this moment.

With every breath, you are reminded that safety and belonging begin within. No matter the shape, size, past wounds or stories held within your cells - your body is worthy of love, of gentleness, of reverence.

I AM
At Home In My Body

Signature Mini Ritual

Apply lotion or oil slowly to your hands, feet or belly with care. Feel each movement as sacred. Say the affirmation aloud.

Soul Reflection

1. What parts of my body have I struggled to feel at home in - and how can I begin to offer them more compassion and care?

2. How do I honour the wisdom of my body when it speaks through sensation, emotion or intuition?

3. What practices help me feel more rooted, present and lovingly connected to the home that is my body?

ALLOW YOUR SOUL TO SPEAK WITHOUT OVER THINKING

I Remain Steady Even As The World Shifts Around Me

This affirmation is a quiet reassurance in the midst of transition. Life is always shifting - seasons change, emotions rise and paths evolve. But within you lives a steady presence that remains untouched.

This whisper reminds syeou to connect with that inner core, to breathe deeply and trust your ability to move with grace. You do not have to have all the answers. You only need to stay present, anchored in your breath and body. Even when everything changes, you can remain grounded, centred and whole. You are the stillness within the storm.

I AM
Steady Amid Change

Signature Mini Ritual

Close your eyes and gently sway from side to side, then return to your centre. Inhale strength. Exhale surrender.

Soul Reflection

1. What inner strengths help me stay grounded when the world around me feels uncertain or fast-moving?

2. How can I honour both my need for stability and my natural ability to adapt and grow through change?

3. When faced with change, what personal rituals, affirmations or reminders help me return to my steady centre?

ALLOW YOUR SOUL TO SPEAK WITHOUT OVER THINKING

I Trust My Inner Knowing To Guide Me

This affirmation invites you to stand in your truth with quiet strength. Your truth does not need to be loud to be powerful - it simply needs to be honoured. This is the voice of your soul, the knowing that lives beneath fear and outside of comparison. When you root into your truth, you create a foundation that is unshakable. You stop seeking validation and begin trusting your inner compass.

This whisper reminds you: you are allowed to take up space. Your truth matters. Let it guide you like the deep roots of an ancient tree.

I AM
Rooted In My Truth

Signature Mini Ritual

Place your hands on your lower belly. Breathe deeply. Say the affirmation slowly with each exhale.

Soul Reflection

1. What does my inner truth feel like - and how can I tell when I am living in alignment with it?

2. When have I trusted my inner knowing, even when it was difficult - and what did that teach me?

3. How can I strengthen my relationship with my intuition and create a life that honours my deepest truths?

ALLOW YOUR SOUL TO SPEAK WITHOUT OVER THINKING

Calm Is My Foundation – I Build My Life Upon It

This affirmation brings you into a space of deep inner clarity. When your mind feels scattered or your energy unsettled, this is a call to return to calm. It reminds you that clarity does not come from control - it comes from stillness. When you ground into your body and breath, the noise begins to quiet. The fog lifts.

This whisper encourages you to slow down, to centre and to trust the wisdom that arises in stillness. You are not lost. You are simply being invited to pause, ground and listen. Your calm is your power.

I AM
Calm, Clear And Grounded

Soul Reflection

1. What practices, places or people help me return to a state of calm clarity when life feels overwhelming?

2. How does being calm and grounded influence the way I make decisions or navigate challenges?

3. What small daily choices can I make to nurture a strong, steady foundation of inner peace?

ALLOW YOUR SOUL TO SPEAK WITHOUT OVER THINKING

Soul Whisper 1 - Reflection Overview

As you close this grounding section, take a moment to reflect on the roots you planted. These final prompts invite you to honour the stability, presence and trust that now live more fully within you - and to carry this steady foundation into the rest of your journey.

1. What practices, people or places help me feel deeply grounded and safe in myself?

2. How has my relationship with presence and stillness evolved through this section?

3. What does being rooted in trust - in life, in myself - look and feel like for me now?

MANTRA: I RETURN TO MY ROOTS. I AM SAFE, STEADY AND SUPPORTED

I AM OPEN

CREATIVITY, FLOW, EMOTIONAL EASE

I Allow The River Of Life To Move Through Me Freely

This affirmation invites you to soften your grip and trust the current of life. When you stop resisting and start allowing, you return to a natural rhythm - one of ease, surrender and grace. Life does not need to be forced.

This whisper reminds you that flow is a state of harmony between doing and being. Even when things feel uncertain, you can ride the wave instead of fighting it. Breathe, release and open. The more you let go, the more life flows through you, guiding you exactly where you need to be.

I AM
Open To Life's Flow

Signature Mini Ritual

Run warm water over your hands or feet and imagine all resistance washing away. Say the affirmation aloud as you dry off.

Soul Reflection

1. Where in my life am I holding back from the natural flow - and what might happen if I surrendered a little more?

2. How does it feel in my body and spirit when I allow life to move through me without resistance?

3. What practices help me trust the unfolding of my journey, even when I cannot see the whole path?

ALLOW YOUR SOUL TO SPEAK WITHOUT OVER THINKING

Inspiration Moves Through Me With Ease And Delight

This affirmation awakens your inner creator. You are a sacred vessel - unique, expressive and filled with untapped magic. Creativity is not just painting or poetry; it is the way you solve problems, make decisions and show up in the world. When you create, you tap into something larger than yourself.

This whisper invites you to release judgment and let your inner flow rise freely. There is no right way - only your way. Your creativity is sacred. Let it be raw, playful and real. Let it move through you and shape something beautiful.

I AM
A Vessel For Creativity

Signature Mini Ritual

Set a timer for five minutes. Free-write or doodle without lifting your pen. Allow whatever comes through to flow.

Soul Reflection

1. When do I feel most alive, inspired and creatively free - and how can I invite more of those moments into my life?

2. What helps me stay open to inspiration without forcing or controlling the creative process?

3. In what ways can I nurture my creative spirit with more ease, joy and self-compassion?

ALLOW YOUR SOUL TO SPEAK WITHOUT OVER THINKING

I Welcome My Emotions As Sacred Messengers

This affirmation invites you to honour the wisdom of your emotions. Your feelings are not flaws - they are messengers guiding you toward truth and healing. To be in tune with them is to listen without judgment, to respond with compassion.

This whisper reminds you that emotional awareness brings balance, depth and presence. When you stop resisting what you feel, your emotions become your teachers - not your burdens. You are allowed to feel. You are allowed to understand yourself through your emotional landscape. Let this whisper guide you into emotional clarity and heart connection.

I AM
In Tune With My Emotions

***

Signature Mini Ritual

Place your hands on your heart. Name aloud what you are feeling in this moment. Say the affirmation as an embrace.

Soul Reflection

1. What emotions have I been resisting - and what might they be trying to lovingly teach me?

2. How can I create a safe space within myself to feel, honour and express my emotions without judgement?

3. When I listen closely, what wisdom or guidance do my emotions offer about my true needs and desires?

ALLOW YOUR SOUL TO SPEAK WITHOUT OVER THINKING

Joy Rises In Me Like The Morning Sun

This affirmation celebrates your inner light. Joy is not something you must earn - it already lives within you. When you make space for joy, you welcome life more fully. It might arrive quietly - in laughter, in sunlight, in moments of peace. Or it might burst forth like a dance. However it comes, joy heals.

This whisper reminds you that joy is not frivolous - it is a sacred part of your wholeness. Let yourself shine, even in small ways. You are allowed to glow, to feel good, to delight in life. Your joy is medicine - for you and the world.

I AM
Radiant With Joy

Signature Mini Ritual

Put on a favourite piece of music. Move or sway slowly with it, smiling softly. Speak the affirmation aloud.

Soul Reflection

1. What simple moments or memories ignite genuine joy within me - and how can I welcome more of them into my days?

2. How does it feel in my body, mind and spirit when I allow myself to fully experience joy without holding back?

3. In what ways can I become a vessel for joy - not just for myself, but for those around me?

ALLOW YOUR SOUL TO SPEAK WITHOUT OVER THINKING

My Feelings Are Valid – I Honour What Lives Within Me

This affirmation offers gentle permission to be fully, authentically you. It reminds you that your feelings, your voice and your truth are worthy of being seen and heard. Expression is a release-it clears stuck energy and brings you home to yourself. Whether you speak, move, write or cry, your emotions deserve space.

This whisper encourages you to share from your heart without fear of judgement. You are safe to be real. You are safe to be soft. When you express what lives within, you reclaim your power and invite deeper connection.

I AM
Safe To Feel And Express

Signature Mini Ritual

Sit quietly and place your hand over your belly. Breathe deeply into it. Whisper the affirmation with each exhale.

Soul Reflection

1. When have I felt truly safe to express my feelings - and what made that space feel supportive?

2. How can I remind myself that all my emotions are valid and worthy of being acknowledged?

3. What gentle practices help me honour and release what lives within me, rather than holding it inside?

ALLOW YOUR SOUL TO SPEAK WITHOUT OVER THINKING

My Spirit Dances In Freely - I Honour My Joy

This affirmation reconnects you with the wild, joyful parts of yourself that may have been quieted. Playfulness is healing. Passion is vitality. Freedom is your birthright.

This whisper reminds you that you do not need permission to explore, to laugh, to follow your curiosity. You are not here to be confined - you are here to feel alive. Let your inner child dance. Let your passions guide your path. You are not too much. You are not too late. You are perfectly placed to live with wonder, with fire and with full-bodied freedom.

I AM
Playful, Passionate And Free

Signature Mini Ritual

Skip, sway or dance freely for two minutes - no rules. Laugh if you need to. End by whispering the affirmation.

Soul Reflection

1. When do I feel most playful and free - and how can I invite more of that energy into my life?

2. What passions light me up from within and how do they connect me to my true self?

3. How can I honour the joy of simply being me, without needing to prove or perfect anything?

ALLOW YOUR SOUL TO SPEAK WITHOUT OVER THINKING

I Open My Heart And Hands To Life's Blessings

This affirmation invites you to soften into receptivity. You have been giving, holding, doing - but now, you are asked to receive. Love, support, rest, abundance - it is all here, waiting.

This whisper reminds you that receiving is not weakness; it is balance. It is an act of trust. You do not have to earn your worthiness. You are already worthy of good things. Open your hands, open your heart. Let the flow come in. Receiving with grace means honouring your needs, saying yes to support and allowing life to care for you, just as you care for others.

I AM
Open To Receive With Grace

Signature Mini Ritual

Sit with palms open and facing upward. Breathe deeply. Whisper the affirmation three times, then write down three things you are ready to receive.

Soul Reflection

1. Where in my life am I being invited to soften and receive, rather than strive and chase?

2. How does it feel in my heart and body when I allow myself to receive with openness and gratitude?

3. What old beliefs about receiving am I ready to release, so I can welcome life's blessings more fully?

ALLOW YOUR SOUL TO SPEAK WITHOUT OVER THINKING

Soul Whisper 2 - Reflection Overview

At the end of this section, these prompts invite you to gently reflect on how you have opened - to emotion, creativity and flow. Let this be a space to honour what has been softened, expressed or released and to welcome the freedom now flowing through you.

1. Where in my life am I opening more fully - to emotion, to inspiration, to possibility?

2. What creative or emotional expressions have surfaced and how have I welcomed them?

3. How can I continue to move with life's flow rather than resist it - by staying open to change and trusting the process?

MANTRA: I OPEN WITH EASE. I WELCOME FLOW, FEELING AND POSSIBILITY

I AM EMPOWERED

CONFIDENCE, COURAGE, BOUNDARIES

I Choose The Path I Walk And The Story I Write

This affirmation reminds you that your story is yours to write. You are not bound by past chapters or others' expectations - you have the power to choose, shift and begin again. Every thought, action and belief is a brushstroke on the canvas of your life.

This whisper invites you to take ownership of your journey with clarity and intention. You are not powerless; you are the storyteller, the creator, the guide. Let this be your invitation to step forward boldly, to edit what no longer serves and to write the life that reflects your deepest truth.

I AM
The Author Of My Life

Signature Mini Ritual

Light a candle and write one sentence declaring a choice you are ready to make. Read it aloud with the affirmation.

Soul Reflection

1. What stories have I been telling myself about who I am - and which ones am I ready to rewrite?

2. What choices can I make today that align with the life and path I truly desire?

3. If I am the author of my life, what new chapter am I ready to begin writing?

ALLOW YOUR SOUL TO SPEAK WITHOUT OVER THINKING

I Take The First Step With Courage, Not Certainty

This affirmation is a gentle nudge forward, reminding you that beginnings do not require certainty - only courage. Starting something new, healing an old wound or stepping toward your dreams can feel daunting but your bravery lies in taking that first step. You do not need a full plan. You do not need to feel ready.

This whisper encourages you to honour your desire and trust your resilience. Each beginning holds magic and momentum. You are capable. You are guided. Let your heart lead. Even the smallest step forward is a sacred act of self-belief.

I AM
Brave Enough To Begin

Signature Mini Ritual

Stand tall, take one step forward intentionally. Whisper the affirmation as you move. Repeat three times.

Soul Reflection

1. What new beginning is calling to me - and what small, courageous step can I take toward it today?

2. How can I honour my bravery, even when the path ahead feels unclear?

3. When in my life have I taken a first step without knowing the outcome - and what did it teach me about myself?

ALLOW YOUR SOUL TO SPEAK WITHOUT OVER THINKING

I Honour The Dreams That Live Within Me

This affirmation honours the sacredness of your longings. Your desires are not selfish or too much - they are soul-messages, pointing you toward alignment and fulfilment.

This whisper invites you to stop shrinking, stop explaining and start allowing. Worthiness is not earned - it is remembered. When you honour what you truly want, you affirm your value and honour your path. Let this whisper be permission to dream, to want deeply and to believe you are enough to receive it. Your desires matter. Your dreams are divine. You are worthy of them all.

I AM
Worthy Of My Desires

Signature Mini Ritual

Write down one desire you have been ignoring. Place it under a crystal or cup overnight. Say the affirmation before sleep.

Soul Reflection

1. What dreams or desires have I tucked away - and how can I begin to honour them today?

2. Where do old stories of "not enough" still linger and how can I gently rewrite them with worthiness and love?

3. What would change in my life if I truly believed I was worthy of all that my heart longs for?

ALLOW YOUR SOUL TO SPEAK WITHOUT OVER THINKING

I Carry Quiet Confidence In All I Do

This affirmation reconnects you with the steady flame within. Confidence does not come from outside approval - it grows from self-trust, inner knowing and authenticity. You do not need to prove yourself to feel powerful.

This whisper invites you to root into your own strength, to remember who you are beneath fear and doubt. You have already walked through storms and risen. Let your confidence rise from your roots - quiet, unwavering, real. You belong. You are capable. You are grounded in your worth. It is from that place, you can rise with grace and power.

I AM
Rooted In Confidence

Signature Mini Ritual

Practice a power pose in front of a mirror. Breathe deeply and say the affirmation three times with a steady gaze.

Soul Reflection

1. What does true, quiet confidence feel like in my body and spirit - and how can I nurture more of it each day?

2. When have I trusted myself and acted from a place of inner strength rather than needing external approval?

3. How can I root deeper into my own worth and allow confidence to rise naturally from within me?

ALLOW YOUR SOUL TO SPEAK WITHOUT OVER THINKING

I Release The Pressure To Be Anything But Myself

This affirmation is a soft, steady truth that asks nothing of you but your presence. You do not need to change, achieve or be anyone other than who you are. Right now, in this breath, you are enough.

This whisper dissolves the pressure to perform or perfect and gently reminds you of your inherent worth. You are worthy of love, rest, joy and belonging - without needing to earn it. Let this whisper hold you when self-doubt creeps in. You are whole. You are seen. You are enough, simply because you are.

I AM
Enough, Just As I Am

ENOUGH

Signature Mini Ritual

Place your hand on your heart and inhale. Say: "I am enough." Exhale and feel the truth settle in.

Soul Reflection

1. Where in my life have I been striving for approval - and what would it feel like to simply be enough?

2. What parts of myself am I ready to embrace with more compassion, without needing to change or improve?

3. How can I honour my worthiness by simply recognising the wholeness already within me?

ALLOW YOUR SOUL TO SPEAK WITHOUT OVER THINKING

My Strength Is Fierce - My Softness Is Sacred

This affirmation celebrates the sacred duality within you. You can be both soft and strong, fierce and tender, grounded and wild. You do not have to choose.

This whisper invites you to honour your complexity - your power that roars and your compassion that heals. You are a force, not because you dominate but because you embody your truth with grace. Let your fire burn bright and let your gentleness be your guide. You are not either/or - you are everything - the storm and the calm, the strength and the sanctuary.

I AM
A Fierce And Gentle Force

Signature Mini Ritual

Hold something soft in one hand and something solid in the other.
Close your eyes and repeat the affirmation, feeling balance.

Soul Reflection

1. How do my strength and my softness work together to support and empower me?

2. When have I honoured both my fierce determination and my tender heart - and how did it feel?

3. How can I give myself permission to be both powerful and gentle in the way I show up for myself and others?

ALLOW YOUR SOUL TO SPEAK WITHOUT OVER THINKING

I Protect My Energy With Love And Boundaries

This affirmation is a boundary drawn in light - not to push others away, but to protect your peace. Clarity is power. When you know what honours your energy and what drains it, you can move through life with intention and integrity.

This whisper reminds you that it is not selfish to have limits - it is self-respect. You are allowed to say no. You are allowed to walk away. You are allowed to choose what supports your soul. Let this clarity anchor you. You get to decide what enters your sacred space.

I AM
Clear On What I Will And Will Not Allow

Signature Mini Ritual

Draw a circle around you (physically or visually). Declare three things you allow in and three you keep out.

Soul Reflection

1. How do my strength and my softness work together to support and empower me?

2. When have I honoured both my fierce determination and my tender heart - and how did it feel?

3. How can I give myself permission to be both powerful and gentle in the way I show up for myself and others?

ALLOW YOUR SOUL TO SPEAK WITHOUT OVER THINKING

Soul Whisper 3 - Reflection Overview

As this empowering section comes to a close, these reflections help you recognise the courage you have embodied, the boundaries you have honoured and the confidence you have reclaimed. Pause here to celebrate your inner strength and the self-respect you have cultivated.

1. What helps me feel empowered and able to stand fully in my truth - even when it feels uncomfortable, unfamiliar or unseen by others?

2. Where have I set or reinforced boundaries that honour my energy and worth?

3. How has courage shown up in my life, even in quiet or unexpected ways?

MANTRA: I STAND IN MY STRENGTH. I CHOOSE MY PATH WITH COURAGE

I AM LOVE

COMPASSION, CONNECTION, SELF-WORTH

Love Flows Through Me And From Me With Ease

This affirmation reminds you of your essence - pure, radiant love. You are not separate from love; you are an embodiment of it. Your presence, your kindness, your being is a living expression of love's infinite forms.

This whisper invites you to recognise that love is not only something to give or receive - it is something you are. Let it flow through your words, your actions and your stillness. When you embody love, you become a source of healing and light in the world. No performance needed. Simply by being, you are love in motion.

I AM
Love In Human Form

Signature Mini Ritual

Place both hands on your heart. Breathe in gently and smile softly. Whisper this affirmation three times as you exhale.

Soul Reflection

1. How do I experience love flowing through me - in my thoughts, my actions and my presence?

2. What practices help me stay connected to the truth that I am already love, not something separate from it?

3. How can I offer love more freely - to myself, to others and to the world - without conditions or expectations?

ALLOW YOUR SOUL TO SPEAK WITHOUT OVER THINKING

I Am Enough And I Am Deeply Loved

This affirmation is a warm embrace for the parts of you that have ever felt unseen, unchosen or unworthy. It gently dissolves old stories of rejection and reminds you that you do not have to change to be loved. You belong - not because of what you do but because of who you are.

This whisper invites you to open your heart, even tenderly, to the truth that love was never meant to be earned. You are inherently lovable. You are enough. You are held in the great web of belonging.

I AM
Worthy Of Love And Belonging

Signature Mini Ritual

Light a candle and sit quietly. Say the affirmation aloud while looking into a mirror or holding a soft object.

Soul Reflection

1. Where in my life have I felt a true sense of love and belonging - and how can I nurture more of that connection?

2. What old stories about my worthiness am I ready to release so I can fully receive love as my birthright?

3. How can I remind myself each day that I am enough and that love surrounds and lives within me?

ALLOW YOUR SOUL TO SPEAK WITHOUT OVER THINKING

I Meet Myself And Others With Gentleness

This affirmation calls you to walk gently in the world - with yourself and with others. Compassion is not just a feeling - it is how you move through life, how you respond to suffering with presence, not judgement.

This whisper reminds you that compassion begins within: in the way you speak to yourself, in the grace you offer your own imperfections. When you embody compassion, you become a balm for others too. Your presence becomes healing. You do not need to fix everything. Just show up, open-hearted. Let your kindness ripple outward.

I AM
Compassion In Motion

Signature Mini Ritual

Write a forgiveness letter to yourself or someone else (you do not need to send it). Breathe in peace. Exhale release.

Soul Reflection

1. How can I meet myself with more gentleness, especially in moments when I feel vulnerable or imperfect?

2. What does it look like to extend true compassion to others while still honouring my own boundaries?

3. How can I embody compassion not just in my thoughts, but in my actions, words and everyday presence?

ALLOW YOUR SOUL TO SPEAK WITHOUT OVER THINKING

My Heart Is Open To Meaningful Connection

This affirmation honours your sacred ability to connect - with self, others and something greater. You are not here to walk alone. Connection is nourishment for the soul, a remembering of our shared humanity.

This whisper reminds you that through authenticity, presence and vulnerability, you become a bridge - between hearts, between realms, between what is and what could be. You are not broken or separate. You are woven into the fabric of life. Trust that the love you send out returns to you, often in ways more beautiful than imagined.

I AM
A Channel For Connection

Signature Mini Ritual

Think of someone you feel grateful for. Hold them in your heart and send them silent thanks.

Soul Reflection

1. What helps me open my heart to authentic, soul-nourishing connections with others?

2. Where in my life am I being called to deepen connection - with myself, with others or with the world around me?

3. How can I stay grounded and true to myself while also remaining open to meaningful relationships and experiences?

ALLOW YOUR SOUL TO SPEAK WITHOUT OVER THINKING

I Honour My Losses With Tenderness And Care

This affirmation is a hand on your heart in times of sorrow. It honours the sacredness of grief and asks you to meet it not with resistance but with gentleness. Grief is not something to rush or fix - it is something to move through with tenderness and breath.

This whisper reminds you that your sorrow is valid tend that healing comes in waves. You are allowed to feel, to cry, to rest. Be gentle with yourself. Let your grief be witnessed, held and honoured. There is beauty in your breaking and strength in your softness.

I AM
Gentle With My Grief

Signature Mini Ritual

Light a small tealight and name aloud a loss you are still holding.
Place your hand on your chest and say the affirmation.

Soul Reflection

1. How can I create space to honour my grief without rushing or
   needing to "fix" it?

2. What would it feel like to meet my losses with tenderness, just as
   they are, without judgment?

3. In what ways has grief shaped my heart - and how can I carry those
   experiences with compassion and grace?

ALLOW YOUR SOUL TO SPEAK WITHOUT OVER THINKING

My Softness Is Not Weakness – It Is Sacred Strength

This affirmation reminds you that softness is not weakness - it is a profound strength. To remain open-hearted in a world that often demands hardness is a radical act. You can hold boundaries and be kind. You can be fierce and still tender.

This whisper invites you to embrace both aspects of yourself: the warrior and the healer, the protector and the nurturer. Your softness allows you to feel deeply; your strength allows you to stand tall. You are not one or the other. You are both and that is powerful.

I AM
Soft Yet Strong

Signature Mini Ritual

Wrap yourself in a soft blanket or shawl. Whisper the affirmation aloud while swaying gently.

Soul Reflection

1. How has my softness been a source of strength in my life, even when it may have been misunderstood?

2. What beliefs about strength am I ready to redefine in a way that honours both my tenderness and resilience?

3. How can I move through the world with both open-hearted softness and unwavering inner strength?

ALLOW YOUR SOUL TO SPEAK WITHOUT OVER THINKING

I Am Never Alone – Love Surrounds Me

This affirmation is a sacred reassurance - you are never alone. Even in your most fragile moments, love surrounds you. It lives in the unseen, in the breath, in the quiet moments when you place your hand on your heart.

This whisper invites you to lean into that love, to trust that you are held - by spirit, by source, by the very fabric of life. You do not have to carry everything alone. You are supported. You are cherished. Let yourself rest in the arms of love, knowing that it is always with you, within you, around you.

I AM
Held In Love, Always

Signature Mini Ritual

Envision yourself embraced by the love of the universe, ancestors, friends. Let the affirmation be a mantra.

Soul Reflection

1. When in my life have I truly felt held and supported by love - seen or unseen?

2. How can I open my heart to feel the presence of love even in moments of loneliness or uncertainty?

3. What practices or reminders help me stay connected to the knowing that I am always surrounded by love?

ALLOW YOUR SOUL TO SPEAK WITHOUT OVER THINKING

Soul Whisper 4 - Reflection Overview

This closing reflection offers space to witness how love has deepened - within you and around you. Let these prompts guide you in honouring the compassion you have extended, the connection you have nurtured and the self-worth you have embraced.

1. What does it mean to love and accept myself fully, right here and now?

2. How do I offer and receive love - and how has that shifted through this section?

3. Where have I deepened connection - within myself or with others - and how has that connection supported my growth or healing?

MANTRA: I AM LOVE, I AM LOVED. I BELONG TO MYSELF AND TO THE WHOLE

I AM EXPRESSIVE

My Voice Is Clear, Kind And Powerful

This affirmation invites you to honour the sacredness of your voice - the pure expression of your soul's truth. Speaking your truth is not about being loud; it is about being real. It is about choosing words that are rooted in authenticity, kindness and self-respect. Your voice matters. Your feelings, your needs and your dreams deserve to be heard.

This whisper reminds you that true power comes from clarity and compassion. When you free your voice, you free your spirit. Trust that the world needs what only you can say - and that when you speak with heart, you speak with light.

I AM
Free To Speak My Truth

Signature Mini Ritual

Inhale deeply and exhale with sound - sigh, hum or tone. Do this three times, then speak the affirmation aloud.

Soul Reflection

1. What truths within me are ready to be spoken with clarity, kindness and courage?

2. How can I honour my voice without fear, trusting that what I have to say matters?

3. When have I spoken my truth and felt empowered - and how can I build on that strength today?

ALLOW YOUR SOUL TO SPEAK WITHOUT OVER THINKING

My Voice Matters - My Story Is Sacred

This affirmation affirms a deep truth: you are worthy of being witnessed, honoured and valued just as you are. Your voice is not too small, too much or insignificant - it carries the weight of your experiences, your wisdom and your heart. Your story is sacred because it is yours and every chapter holds meaning.

This whisper invites you to stand in your truth, trusting that you are seen beyond the surface, heard beyond the words and valued beyond measure. When you honour your own story, you invite others to meet you in that sacred recognition.

I AM
Heard, Seen And Valued

Signature Mini Ritual

Stand in front of a mirror. Place your hand on your throat and say the affirmation slowly and clearly.

Soul Reflection

1. Where in my life have I felt truly heard, seen and valued - and how did that experience shape me?

2. How can I honour and value my own voice and story, even when others may not fully understand it?

3. What would it feel like to move through the world knowing that my presence and my story are sacred gifts?

ALLOW YOUR SOUL TO SPEAK WITHOUT OVER THINKING

I Speak With Intention, Not Apology

This affirmation invites you to honour your needs and desires without guilt, shame or hesitation. Clarity is a gift you give yourself - and the world. When you know what you need, you can stand in your truth with strength and grace. You no longer shrink, second-guess or explain away your worth.

This whisper reminds you that it is not selfish to speak your needs with intention; it is an act of self-respect and self-trust. Your voice is a powerful tool for setting boundaries, expressing dreams and shaping the life you are here to live. Speak it with clarity and courage.

I AM
Clear In What I Need And Desire

Signature Mini Ritual

Write down one need or boundary. Speak it aloud with confidence while looking in the mirror.

Soul Reflection

1. What am I currently needing or desiring - and how can I express it with intention, not apology?

2. Where in my life have I been holding back my truth - and what would it feel like to speak it clearly and confidently?

3. How does it feel in my body and spirit when I honour my voice and communicate from a place of clarity and self-worth?

ALLOW YOUR SOUL TO SPEAK WITHOUT OVER THINKING

What I Express From The Heart Creates Connection

This affirmation invites you to trust the power of honest, heart-led communication. When you speak from your truth, without masks or fear, you create spaces where real connection can blossom. Honesty is not harshness - it is authenticity woven with compassion.

This whisper reminds eyou that your words have the power to heal, to bridge and to deepen relationships when they rise from the heart. You are not here to silence your feelings or diminish your voice. You are a sacred vessel for honest expression and through your truth, you invite others to stand bravely in theirs.

I AM
A Vessel Of Honest
Expression

Signature Mini Ritual

Journal one page without censoring. Let the words move through you. End by reading aloud a line that resonates.

Soul Reflection

1. When have I shared something honestly from my heart - and how did it deepen my connection with another or with myself?

2. What truths within me are ready to be expressed with openness, vulnerability and love?

3. How can I create more space in my life to speak and live from the heart, trusting that honesty invites true connection?

ALLOW YOUR SOUL TO SPEAK WITHOUT OVER THINKING

Every Part Of Me Belongs In My Story

This affirmation is a loving reminder that your story, in all its beauty and imperfection, is sacred. Every experience, every emotion, every chapter has shaped the soul you are today. Nothing needs to be erased or hidden.

This whisper invites you to embrace your whole self - the messy parts, the victories, the quiet moments - as threads of a rich and worthy tapestry. Your story matters because you matter. When you honour your journey without judgment, you reclaim your voice and your power. You are not broken or incomplete; you are a living, breathing story of resilience, love and becoming.

I AM
A Story Worth Telling

Signature Mini Ritual

Choose a photo, object or song that reminds you of a personal moment. Tell yourself its story aloud.

Soul Reflection

1. What parts of my journey have I hidden or dismissed - and how might it feel to welcome them into my story with compassion?

2. How does it shift my sense of self when I view every chapter of my life as sacred and worthy of being told?

3. If I were to honour my full story - the struggles, the triumphs, the quiet moments - what truth would I want the world to hear?

ALLOW YOUR SOUL TO SPEAK WITHOUT OVER THINKING

I Express Myself Without Fear Or Performance

This affirmation is a call to stand fully in the truth of who you are. Authenticity is not about being perfect - it is about being real, without masking, without performing and without shrinking to fit someone else's expectations.

This whisper reminds you that your truest expression is your greatest strength. When you speak, create and live from your authentic self, you invite deeper connection, greater freedom and genuine joy. You are not here to be a version of yourself for approval - you are here to be courageously, unapologetically you. Your authenticity is your light and your courage lets it shine.

I AM
Courageously Authentic

Signature Mini Ritual

Dress, speak or move in a way that feels like you. Take a deep breath and affirm your truth.

Soul Reflection

1. What parts of myself feel most natural and true - and how can I allow them to shine more freely?

2. Where in my life am I ready to release the need to perform or please and step more fully into my authentic self?

3. How does it feel in my body, mind and spirit when I express myself without fear, simply as I am?

ALLOW YOUR SOUL TO SPEAK WITHOUT OVER THINKING

I Trust What Rises From Within And Give It Voice

This affirmation invites you to honour your inner voice as sacred - your personal channel of soul truth. Within you lives a deep well of wisdom, shaped by your experiences, intuition, ancestral memory and inner knowing. Too often, that voice is quieted by self-doubt, fear or the noise of the outside world.

This whisper is a reclamation. It calls you to pause, listen and speak from that deeper place. You are not lost. You are not unsure. The answers are there, rising softly from within. Trust them. Honour them. When you give voice to your inner wisdom, you empower your path - and inspire others to do the same.

I AM
The Voice Of My Inner Wisdom

Signature Mini Ritual

Sit in silence and ask: "What do I need to hear today?" Write down the first whisper.

Soul Reflection

1. How can I create more space in my life to hear the quiet wisdom that rises from within me?

2. When have I trusted and acted on my inner knowing - and what was the outcome?

3. What practices or intentions help me strengthen my trust in my inner voice and express it with clarity and courage?

ALLOW YOUR SOUL TO SPEAK WITHOUT OVER THINKING

Soul Whisper 5 - Reflection Overview

As you complete this expressive chapter, these prompts invite you to reflect on the truth you have voiced and the freedom found in sharing your authentic self. This is a moment to honour your expression - raw, real and fully yours.

1. What truths within me have risen to the surface and been given voice?

2. Where have I allowed myself to express authentically, without apology?

3. How has using my voice created more freedom, connection or alignment in my life?

MANTRA: I SPEAK WITH TRUTH. MY VOICE IS A SACRED INSTRUMENT OF SOUL

I AM ALIGNED

CLARITY, DISCERNMENT, INSIGHT

I Bring My Energy To What Feels Aligned And True

This affirmation invites you to reclaim your energy and direct it with intention. Not everything deserves your time, your attention or your spirit. This is your reminder to gently release distractions, obligations and expectations that pull you away from your true path. Focus is not about doing more; IT IS about aligning your energy with what nourishes your soul.

This whisper calls you to trust what feels resonant, to say yes to what uplifts you and to let go of what no longer serves. When you focus on what matters most, your life begins to flow with clarity, purpose and grace.

I AM
Focused On What Matters

Signature Mini Ritual

Light a candle and write down your top three priorities. Say the affirmation aloud while gazing into the flame.

Soul Reflection

1. What in my life feels truly aligned with my values, my soul and my deepest truth - and how can I give it more of my energy?

2. Where have I been scattering my energy - and how might I lovingly redirect it toward what matters most to me?

3. How can I create simple daily practices that keep me focused, clear and connected to what feels most true?

ALLOW YOUR SOUL TO SPEAK WITHOUT OVER THINKING

My Intuition Speaks Clearly And I Listen

This affirmation invites you to deepen your relationship with your inner guidance. Your intuition is a quiet, constant presence - always offering insight, direction and truth. It does not shout; it softly rises from within, asking only for your trust and attention. When you slow down and listen, your inner wisdom becomes a clear and steady guide.

This whisper reminds you that you already hold the answers you seek. You are connected to a greater knowing and when you trust that voice within, you move through life with greater confidence, clarity and peace.

I AM
In Tune With My Inner Wisdom

Signature Mini Ritual

Sit in stillness and ask, "What do I need to know right now?" Journal your first impressions.

Soul Reflection

1. When has my intuition guided me in a way that logic alone could not - and what did I learn from trusting it?

2. What practices help me quiet the noise around me so I can hear the clear voice of my inner wisdom?

3. How can I deepen my trust in the quiet nudges, feelings and signs that rise from within me?

ALLOW YOUR SOUL TO SPEAK WITHOUT OVER THINKING

I Trust My Ability To Choose With Clarity And Calm

This affirmation invites you to trust your inner compass. You are capable of making aligned, wise choices without overthinking or spiralling in self-doubt. Clarity does not always come from having all the answers - it often comes from presence, intention and deep self-trust.

This whisper reminds you that your decisions carry power when made from a place of calm and truth. You do not need to rush or second-guess. You are allowed to take up space in your choices, to honour what feels right and to walk forward with confidence. Even a small step made in alignment can shift your entire path. You already know - now trust yourself enough to choose.

I AM
Clear And Decisive

Signature Mini Ritual

Write down a current decision. Take three deep breaths, then circle the option that brings peace.

Soul Reflection

1. When have I made a decision from a place of clarity and calm - and how did that experience strengthen my trust in myself?

2. What fears or doubts tend to cloud my decision-making and how can I gently clear them away?

3. How can I honour the power of small, clear choices that align with my inner truth each day?

ALLOW YOUR SOUL TO SPEAK WITHOUT OVER THINKING

I Align My Actions With My Values

This affirmation invites you to stand firmly in the foundation of your truth. Being grounded in truth means living in alignment with what you believe, value and hold sacred - not just in words, but through your daily choices and actions.

This whisper reminds you that your truth is not something you have to defend or prove; it is something you embody quietly and consistently. When you act from your values, you create a life that feels authentic, stable and whole. Let your truth be the soil you root into, the compass that steadies you and the light that guides your way.

I AM
Grounded In Truth

Signature Mini Ritual

Name aloud three things that matter most to you. Say the affirmation as you plant your feet firmly on the ground.

Soul Reflection

1. What core values guide my life - and how do they show up in the choices I make each day?

2. Where in my life might there be a gap between what I believe and how I act - and how can I gently realign?

3. How does it feel in my body and spirit when I act from a place of integrity and inner truth?

ALLOW YOUR SOUL TO SPEAK WITHOUT OVER THINKING

I Welcome Insight From Both Within And Beyond

This affirmation invites you to soften the walls of certainty and open to the gifts of new understanding. Growth often comes not from holding tighter to what we know, but from allowing fresh perspectives to broaden and enrich our view.

This whisper reminds you that wisdom can arise from unexpected places - through others, through experience and through the quiet voice within. You are not losing yourself by staying open; you are expanding your capacity for truth, compassion and deeper connection. When you welcome insight with curiosity and trust, your path unfolds with greater richness and clarity.

I AM
Open To New Perspectives

Signature Mini Ritual

Turn your journal sideways or upside down. Write a reflection in a new way and see what changes.

Soul Reflection

1. When was the last time a shift in perspective brought clarity, healing or growth into my life?

2. What beliefs or patterns might I be ready to loosen or expand to invite in fresh understanding?

3. How can I stay open to the wisdom that flows through others, nature, synchronicities and my own inner knowing?

ALLOW YOUR SOUL TO SPEAK WITHOUT OVER THINKING

I Let Clarity Come Through Surrender, Not Struggle

This affirmation invites you to trust that you are never walking alone. There is a higher wisdom - whether you call it Source, Spirit, intuition or inner knowing - that gently guides your path. True clarity often does not come from forcing answers or controlling outcomes; it rises naturally when you surrender to the greater flow of life.

This whisper reminds you that surrender is not weakness - it is sacred trust. When you let go of the need to force and instead open to divine timing and guidance, you create space for insight, ease and miracles to find you. You are always supported.

I AM
Guided By A Higher Wisdom

Signature Mini Ritual

Lay down and place one hand on your forehead. Breathe and repeat the affirmation as a gentle mantra.

Soul Reflection

1. What would it feel like to stop pushing for answers and instead allow guidance to arise through stillness and surrender?

2. When have I experienced clarity or direction after letting go of control - and what did that teach me about trust?

3. How can I create more space in my life to receive insight from a higher wisdom, rather than forcing a solution?

ALLOW YOUR SOUL TO SPEAK WITHOUT OVER THINKING

I Receive, Trust And Align With The Messages Of My Soul

This affirmation invites you to become an open, trusting vessel for the wisdom that lives within you. Your soul is always speaking - through intuition, sensation, dreams and quiet inner knowing. When you create space to listen without doubt or distraction, you become a clear channel for that truth to rise and guide you.

This whisper reminds you that your inner truth is not something you must search for; it already exists within. Trust what you receive. Honour what you hear. When you align with your soul's messages, you move through life with deeper purpose, authenticity and peace.

I AM
Guided By A Higher Wisdom

Signature Mini Ritual

Sit with your journal and write a letter from your soul to yourself. Let the words come freely.

Soul Reflection

1. What supports me in becoming a clear, open channel for the wisdom that lives within me?

2. How do I know when a message or nudge is coming from my soul - and how can I honour it with trust?

3. In what ways can I realign my actions and choices to reflect the truth I feel most deeply inside?

ALLOW YOUR SOUL TO SPEAK WITHOUT OVER THINKING

Soul Whisper 6 - Reflection Overview

These closing reflections offer space to acknowledge the clarity and insight that have surfaced through this section. Pause here to feel into your alignment, trusting the guidance that continues to rise from within.

1. What inner insights have surfaced that are helping me align more fully with my truth?

2. Where have I made clear choices or gentle shifts that feel deeply aligned?

3. How does clarity feel in my body, mind and spirit - and how can I nurture it?

MANTRA: I HONOUR MY KNOWING. I MOVE FORWARD WITH CLARITY

I AM CONNECTED

TRUST, PEACE, SACRED AWARENESS

I Am Never Alone - I Walk With The Unseen

This affirmation is a gentle reminder that you are part of something vast, sacred and eternal. Even when you feel alone, you are held - by your ancestors, your guides, the Earth and the unseen forces of love that surround you. You are not separate; you are deeply connected to the web of life.

This whisper invites you to lean into that invisible support, to root yourself in the knowing that you are guided, protected and never walking this path alone. When you trust in something greater, you find strength, meaning and a deeper sense of belonging in every step.

I AM
Rooted In Something Greater

Signature Mini Ritual

Light a candle and call in the presence of ancestors, spirit or higher self. Whisper the affirmation three times.

Soul Reflection

1. When have I felt the quiet presence of something greater holding, guiding or walking beside me?

2. What spiritual or ancestral connections help me feel rooted, supported and part of a larger whole?

3. How can I deepen my awareness of the unseen support around me and draw strength from it in daily life?

ALLOW YOUR SOUL TO SPEAK WITHOUT OVER THINKING

I Align With The Rhythm Of Life

This affirmation invites you to move with life, not against it. Just as the tides flow, the moon cycles and the seasons shift, your life also moves in divine rhythm. Harmony is not about constant peace – it is about trust, timing and presence.

This whisper reminds you that when you release resistance and tune into the greater flow, life meets you with grace. You are part of a cosmic dance not separate from it. By aligning with its rhythm, you invite synchronicity, ease and a deeper sense of connection to all that is. Let life lead. Let yourself move in harmony.

I AM
In Harmony With The Universe

Signature Mini Ritual

Step outside and observe nature's pace - clouds, wind, birds. Repeat the affirmation with your breath.

Soul Reflection

1. What helps me feel attuned to the natural flow and timing of life, rather than pushing against it?

2. Where in my life am I being invited to release resistance and trust in the unfolding path?

3. How can I live more intentionally in harmony with the cycles of nature, energy and my own inner rhythm?

ALLOW YOUR SOUL TO SPEAK WITHOUT OVER THINKING

Every Being I Meet Is A Reflection Of Love

This affirmation invites you to see through the lens of unity - to recognise that beneath all appearances, we are deeply interconnected. Every soul you meet, every moment you share, carries the potential to reflect love, truth and shared humanity.

This whisper is a call to soften separation and remember that we are all part of something greater - woven together by energy, spirit and divine presence. When you live from this awareness, compassion flows more freely, judgment dissolves and your heart expands. You are not separate from the world - you are an essential thread in the sacred web of all that is.

I AM
Connected To All That Is

Signature Mini Ritual

Send a silent blessing to someone you love, someone neutral and someone difficult. Repeat the affirmation.

Soul Reflection

1. How does it shift my perspective when I view others - even in challenge - as mirrors of love and shared humanity?

2. What helps me feel connected to something greater than myself - to people, nature, spirit or the collective whole?

3. How can I show up in the world with more compassion, knowing that we are all threads of the same sacred web?

ALLOW YOUR SOUL TO SPEAK WITHOUT OVER THINKING

Every Being I Meet Is A Reflection Of Love

This affirmation acknowledges your sacred role as a soul who moves between worlds - between the physical and spiritual, the conscious and the intuitive, the earthly and the divine. You are both grounded in this life and attuned to subtle energies beyond it.

This whisper reminds you that your sensitivity is a gift, not a burden. When you honour your connection to both realms, you become a channel for insight, healing and truth. You are a bridge - carrying light between dimensions, messages between hearts and wisdom from the unseen into the here and now. Walk with grace. You belong to both worlds.

I AM
A Bridge Between Realms

Signature Mini Ritual

Sit in silence and visualise a golden bridge connecting you to divine wisdom. Whisper the affirmation slowly.

Soul Reflection

1. When have I sensed or experienced guidance from the unseen - and how did I respond to it?

2. How can I honour my role as a bridge between spiritual and physical worlds in daily, grounded ways?

3. What supports me in staying balanced and graceful as I navigate both intuitive insight and earthly experience?

ALLOW YOUR SOUL TO SPEAK WITHOUT OVER THINKING

I Receive Guidance In Many Forms And I Remain Open

This affirmation reminds you that sacred guidance is always available - whispering through intuition, synchronicities, dreams, signs and even silence. You are never truly without direction; the key is in learning to listen with openness and trust.

This whisper invites you to expand your awareness beyond logic and allow wisdom to reach you in unexpected ways. When you release the need to control how answers arrive, you create space for magic, clarity and divine timing. Stay open-hearted, stay receptive. The Universe speaks to those who listen - not just with their ears, but with their soul.

I AM
Open To Sacred Guidance

Signature Mini Ritual

Pull a card, symbol or message at random (from nature, books or divination). Journal its meaning.

Soul Reflection

1. What are some of the ways sacred guidance has shown up in my life - through intuition, signs, dreams or others?

2. How can I stay open to guidance even when it arrives in unexpected or subtle ways?

3. What helps me discern between fear and true inner guidance and how can I deepen that trust?

ALLOW YOUR SOUL TO SPEAK WITHOUT OVER THINKING

I Trust Life's Unfolding And My Place Within It

This affirmation is an invitation to soften into the natural rhythm of life - to trust that you are exactly where you need to be, even if the path is not clear. When you release resistance and let go of the need to control, you begin to feel the gentle current that is always been carrying you.

This whisper reminds you that life is not something you have to force or chase – it is something you can move with. Even in uncertainty, there is wisdom. Even in stillness, there is progress. You are not separate from the flow; you are part of it. Trust it. Breathe with it.

I AM
One With The Flow Of Life

Signature Mini Ritual

Journal your current season of life using river imagery. Speak the affirmation aloud while slowly tracing your breath.

Soul Reflection

1. Where in my life am I being invited to release control and trust the natural rhythm of becoming?

2. What helps me feel connected to the greater flow - even when things don't go as planned?

3. How can I deepen my trust in life's timing, knowing that I am exactly where I need to be?

ALLOW YOUR SOUL TO SPEAK WITHOUT OVER THINKING

I Open My Being To Radiate Kindness And Compassion

This affirmation calls you to remember the radiant essence of who you are. At your core, you are light. You are love. And when you move through the world with an open heart, you become a vessel for healing - not just for yourself, but for others too.

This whisper reminds you that your energy has impact. Every kind word, every gentle act, every moment of compassion ripples outward in ways you may never fully see. You do not need to force or fix; simply allow your presence to be a blessing. When you open to love, love flows through you. When you shine, others remember their own light.

I AM
A Channel for Light And Love

Signature Mini Ritual

Place your hands in a prayer position at your heart, then slowly open them outward. Say the affirmation and imagine sending love into the world.

Soul Reflection

1. How can I become a clearer channel for love and light in my thoughts, actions and presence today?

2. What helps me stay open-hearted and compassionate, even when it feels difficult or uncomfortable?

3. In what ways can I radiate kindness - not just toward others, but also inward, toward myself?

ALLOW YOUR SOUL TO SPEAK WITHOUT OVER THINKING

Soul Whisper 7 - Reflection Overview

At the end of this sacred section, take time to honour the connections that have deepened - with spirit, self and all that is. These prompts support you in recognising the quiet peace and divine trust now anchoring your path.

1. How do I experience connection - to spirit, nature, others or the unseen?

2. Where has a sense of peace or sacred presence emerged more fully in my life - and how can I continue to nurture and make space for it?

3. What helps me trust the invisible threads that weave my life with greater meaning?

MANTRA: I TRUST THE UNSEEN. I WALK IN PEACE WITH LIFE, SPIRIT AND SELF

SOUL WHISPER 8

I AM WHOLE

INTEGRATION, EXPANSION, SOUL COMPLETION

I Honour How Far I've Come And Trust Where I'm Going

This affirmation invites you to pause and honour the sacred path you have walked - every step, every lesson, every moment of becoming. You are not the same person who began this journey. You have grown, softened, risen and remembered.

This whisper is a gentle reminder that while the future may still be unfolding, you can trust its rhythm. You carry wisdom now - earned through experience and felt through the heart. Let yourself acknowledge your resilience. Let yourself believe in what is ahead. The journey is not about perfection; it is about presence, faith and the courage to keep going. You are guided. You are ready. You are exactly where you need to be.

I AM
Trusting My Journey

Signature Mini Ritual

Light a candle and place a hand on your heart. Say the affirmation while breathing into a memory that shaped you.

Soul Reflection

1. What milestones or inner shifts am I most proud of on my journey so far - and how can I pause to honour them today?

2. Where am I being called to lean into trust, even if I can't yet see the full path ahead?

3. How can I remind myself that every step, even the uncertain ones, is part of a meaningful unfolding?

ALLOW YOUR SOUL TO SPEAK WITHOUT OVER THINKING

I Am Both Complete And Always Becoming

This affirmation honours the sacred truth that you are already whole - nothing missing, nothing broken - while also recognising the endless unfolding of your soul. You are not a project to fix but a being to embrace, expand and express.

This whisper invites you to release the idea that you must "arrive" somewhere to be enough. You already are. And yet, your spirit continues to grow, stretch and awaken into more of itself. Wholeness and expansion are not opposites - they dance together. You are both the rooted tree and the reaching branches. You are the masterpiece and the work in progress. Trust this becoming.

I AM
Whole And Expanding

Signature Mini Ritual

Stand with your arms wide open. Breathe in and visualise yourself as a radiant, expanding mandala. Say the affirmation aloud.

Soul Reflection

1. In what ways can I celebrate my wholeness as I am, even while continuing to grow and evolve?

2. How do I balance self-acceptance with a gentle openness to transformation and new possibilities?

3. What parts of me are ready to expand - not out of lack, but from the fullness of who I already am?

ALLOW YOUR SOUL TO SPEAK WITHOUT OVER THINKING

Everything I Seek Has Always Lived Within Me

This final affirmation is a homecoming - a sacred return to the truth that you have been enough all along. So often, we search outside ourselves for meaning, healing, purpose or love, forgetting that the light we are seeking already burns within.

As you arrive at this final whisper, may you remember: everything sacred you have touched - each affirmation, each breath, each truth - has simply mirrored what has always lived within you. The light you were seeking was never separate. It is you. It always has been - but now, through the awakening of your inner voice, you can truly recognise it.

I AM
The Light I Have Been Looking For

Signature Mini Ritual

Sit in stillness and visualise a light glowing at the centre of your chest. Let it grow and surround you. Whisper the affirmation as a closing blessing.

Soul Reflection

1. What qualities or truths have I spent time seeking externally that already exist within me?

2. How can I reconnect with my inner light and let it guide me, especially in moments of doubt or darkness?

3. In what ways can I honour myself as the source of wisdom, love and light I have been searching for all along?

ALLOW YOUR SOUL TO SPEAK WITHOUT OVER THINKING

Soul Whisper 8 - Reflection Overview

As your journey draws to a close, these final prompts invite you to reflect on all you have integrated and become. Honour the wholeness that has emerged - the quiet expansion, the soul remembrance and the light that now lives more fully within you.

1. How can I honour both how far I have come and how much I continue to become?

2. What aspects of myself feel more integrated, accepted or at peace now?

3. How can I carry the light of this journey forward, as a living part of my daily life?

MANTRA: I AM COMPLETE. I AM EVER-UNFOLDING. I AM HOME

Further Reflections

Further Reflections

GRATITUDE

YOU HEARD THE WHISPER
YOU ANSWERED THE CALL

Thank you for walking this soul-led journey with me through *Whispers to My Soul*.

I hope these whispers have offered you moments of stillness, truth and deeper connection with your inner voice. Every affirmation you speak, every reflection you write and every breath you take in presence is part of your sacred unfolding.

May you continue to honour your emotions, trust your intuition and embrace the quiet wisdom that lives within you.

I am deeply grateful for your time, energy and presence. If this book has resonated with your heart, I would love to hear from you. Your reflections and shared experiences are part of this ever-growing circle of healing and light.

May your path continue to blossom - with grace, clarity and soul-deep remembrance.

PUBLISHED WORLDWIDE

MMXXV

ISBN 978-1-7640433-1-1